Candy & Rigor Mortis

Vol. 3:

Epitaph

By JT Williams & Jorge Mendez

Wider Perspectivesd Publishing ¤ 2024 ¤ Hampton Roads, Va.

1st run released February 2024

Cover art by Jennie Zell
Zellsbells.com

Wider Perspectives Publishing, Hampton Roads, Virginia
ISBN: 978-1-952773-86-0

Dedication

These are not Haiku

They're American Sentence

Thank you, Jeff Hewitt

Content Note

Haiku by "Hacksaw" JT Williams
marked with (JT)

Haiku by Jorge "Carving Knife" Mendez
marked with (JM)

Except that they're American Sentences

Pages (JT)

I bought this cursed book

I literally can't stop

reading the damn thing

Disclaimer (JM)

Oh no, not this book

This book's not cursed…Well, at least

not that I know of

Treat (JT)

You call me creepy

because I like spooky shit

no candy for you

Valentine I (JT)

A man gives his heart

to the woman he loves most

then falls to the floor

Valentine II (JT)

I gave her my heart

I thought that's what she wanted

it was my liver

Rest (JM)

Just take a load off

You will only die tired

if you choose to run

Plight of the Living Dead (JM)

postmortem livin'
ain't all it's cracked up to be
I'm always hungry

Eating brains is hard
The skull is tough to get thru
Hardheaded humans

All food is fast food
I never did like fast food
and I am quite slow

Fhtagh (JT)

Do you have some time

to talk about our savior,

great god Cthulhu?

Sparkle (JM)

Twilight's fuckin' lame

Edward's such a bitch-ass vamp

Someone should stake him

Oops! (JM)

I made a mistake

and Google searched my symptoms

Turns out I been dead

Laughing (JM)

It's all fun and games

until the clown stops smiling

but keeps on laughing

"What's With All the Screaming?" - Jonathon Coulton (JT)

I made a monster

just to get your attention –

they said I was mad

Flame (JT)

I carry a torch

for you like the villagers

did for Frankenstein

Thing in the Closet (JM)

Confronting the thing
living inside my closet
had me so stressed out

I could hear its breath,
heavy, labored, ferocious
from behind the door,

but I finally
decided to face my fear
I took a deep breath,

flung open the door
and there it was, cowering,
seemingly frightened

As it turns out, the
monster had been in hiding
from me all along

ever since that night
I have slept like a baby,
so has the monster

Evil Waze (JT)

I was invited
to a place in the mountains,
so I drove myself

Followed GPS
it brought me to this cabin
then said, "they're waiting"

Bed, Blood-Bath & Beyond (JM)

Electric toaster?

Of course not, don't be silly

It's just a bath bomb

Nec-Romantic (JM)

Um, I am not a

romantic, these candles are

for your sacrifice

Absolved (JT)

Religion teaches
fear – so I won't judge your priests
and your witch trials

Reality Bites (JM)

Damn he's been bitten

I know what I must do now

Better him than me

Survival Tips (JM)

Board up the windows
Use slow people as decoys
Wear some comfy shoes

Seasoning (JM)

When the sun's bedtime
approaches bringing darkness,
light becomes timid

Even shadows hide
fearful of creatures lurking,
waiting, breath baited

for the feast of night,
the wild buffet of moonlight
where nightmares are food

Fear provides flavor
Things taste better when they're scared,
so we marinate.

Donation (JT)

Church sign says become
an organ donor and give
your heart to Jesus

I can't remove mine
so, I, in the name of Christ,
harvested a few

But when I dropped them
in the collection basket
everybody screamed

Nostromo (JT)

Something warm and close

to my heart, then suddenly

it bursts from my chest

Image (JT)

Look in the mirror

What is worse—no reflection

or someone else's?

Envy (JM)

When I heard the news

about the torture and pain

his victims endured

I was furious

How dare he get arrested

before my turn came?

Funny Games (JM)

I find the screaming
so fucking hysterical,
it's a distraction

As if the screaming
will somehow make me spare you
Man, that's a good one

I'm laughing so hard
the tears in my eyes make it
hard to see my prey

Luckily this blade
is so big it's hard to miss
even when they run

Eventually,
they trip on not a damn thing
It's hilarious

You know what they say
You can not have manslaughter
without the 'laughter'

Crush of the Undead (JM)

Been dating this girl

...says she loves me for my brain

Must be a zombie

Consumers (JT)

At the department

store—zombie apocalypse

can't tell which is which

Silver Shamrock (JT)

I bought a clown mask

for this Halloween, but now

I can't take it off

Fido (JM)

Every thirty days

under light of the full moon,

it's the same problem

To put it mildly

my life gets kinda hairy

I'll need a haircut

All my neighbors' pets

have been coming up missing,

but I plead the fifth

It may look fun but,

chasing my tail in circles

makes me so dizzy

I'm covered in fleas,

I'm allergic to silver,

The mailman hates me,

and for some reason

all I want is someone to

call me a good boy

Stroller (JT)

New mother, baby

carriage pushed quickly, distant

screaming from the park

Osh Kosh Kebab (JM)

Might be a bit snug
around the waist, but it will
have to do for now

I'm sure I can find
a looser fitting toddler
sooner or later

I mean, it's not like
you can return a child skin
believe me I've tried

Grave Situation (JT)

I knock forever

Nobody opens the door,

too far down to dig

<u>Final Girl</u> (JM)

I'm a survivor

I got skills to dodge the kills

I'm the final girl

So what I gave up

drugs, sex, fun in general?

I'm alive ain't I?

Relax (JM)

See? I told you so

This book is not cursed at all

Everything is fine

...But Just in Case (JM)

How to end a curse:

It's really quite simple, all

you have to do is…

FIN

FOR MORE HORROR CONTENT BE SURE TO CHECK OUT JT & JORGE'S WEEKLY PODCAST

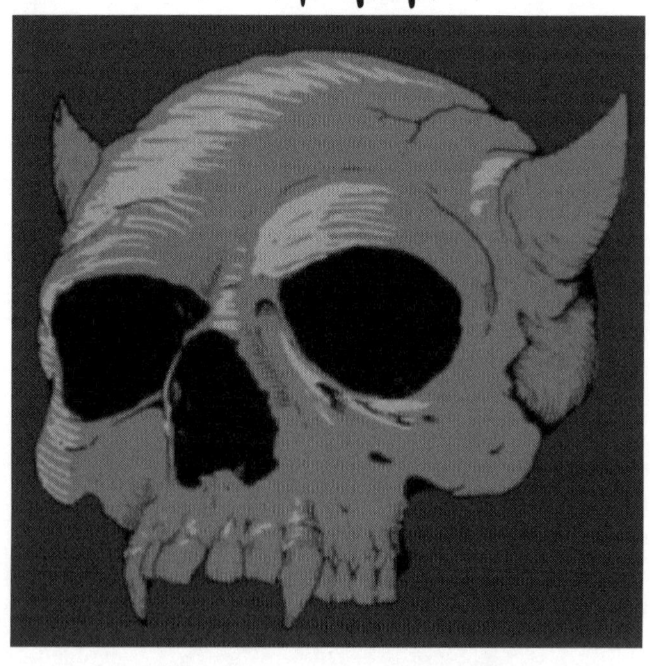

ALSO AVAILABLE

Candy & Rigor Mortis

Vol. 1 & 2

colophon

Brought to you by Wider Perspectives Publishing, care of James Wilson, with the mission of advancing the poetry and creative community of Hampton Roads, Virginia.

This page used to have many cute and poetic expressions, but the sheer number of quality artists deserving mention has superseded the need to art. This has become some serious business; please check out how *They art*...

Patricia Davis
Tabetha Moon House
Nick Marickovich
Grey Hues
Rivers Raye
Madeline Garcia
Chichi Iwuorie
Symay Rhodes
Tanya Cunningham-Jones (Scientific Eve)
Terra Leigh
Raymond M. Simmons
Samantha Borders-Shoemaker
Taz Weysweete'
Jade Leonard
Darean Polk
Bobby K. (The Poor Man's Poet)
J. Scott Wilson (TEECH!)
Charles Wilson
Gloria Darlene Mann
Neil Spirtas
Jorge Mendez & JT Williams
Sarah Eileen Williams
Stephanie Diana (Noftz)
Shanya – Lady S.
Jason Brown (Drk Mtr)
Ken Sutton
Britt Gardner
Faith May Griffin
Arlandria Speaks (Faith Clay)
Kailyn Rae Sasso
Crickyt J. Expression
Se'Mon-Michelle Rosser
Lisa M. Kendrick
Cassandra IsFree
Nich (Nicholis Williams)
Samantha Geovjian Clarke
Natalie Morison-Uzzle
Gus Woodward II
Patsy Bickerstaff
Edith Blake
Jack Cassada
Dezz
M. Antoinette Adams
Catherine TL Hodges
Kent Knowlton
Linda Spence-Howard
Tony Broadway
Zach Crowe
Mark Willoughby
Maria April C.
Vanessa Jones
Martina Champion
... and others to come soon.

the Hampton Roads Artistic Collective (757 Perspectives) & The Poet's Domain are all WPP literary journals in cooperation with Scientific Eve or Live Wire Press

Check for those artists on FaceBook, Instagram, the Virginia Poetry Online channel on YouTube, and other social media.

Made in the USA
Middletown, DE
27 July 2024

58057163R00050